The Wind in the Willows COLLECTION

The Visitors

Story by Geoff Alan
Illustrated by Mark Ripley

Based on a Martin Gates Production © 1996 BMG Entertainment,
Licensed by Just Licensing Limited. All rights reserved.
Published in Great Britain in 1997 by World International Ltd.,
Deanway Technology Centre, Wilmslow Road, Handforth, Cheshire SK9 3FB.
Printed in Finland. ISBN 0 7498 2855 2

All seemed right with the world as Toad sat sipping a cup of tea. He nestled in a large leather armchair within Toad Hall's library.

"Ho-hum!" he yawned. "I've just time for an after-lunch nap before Badger, Mole and Ratty arrive. What a likeable, popular fellow I am!"

As Toad raced outside across the lawn, Rat, Mole and Badger approached. They had just arrived in Rat's boat which he had moored at Toad's nearby boat-house.

"Whatever's wrong?" cried Rat. "You look as if you've seen a ghost!"

Toad rushed past, seeming more startled than ever.

"**S**trange sounds and goings-on," he blurted. "In the library! Keep away, whatever you do!"

"But we came especially to help sort out your books today," called Mole.

Toad turned to beckon the others. Suddenly, he froze, his mouth and eyes wide open.

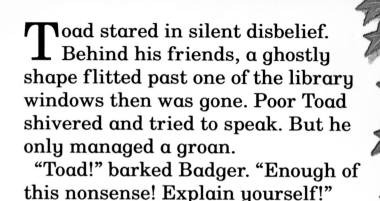

Toad stared in silent disbelief. Behind his friends, a ghostly shape flitted past one of the library windows then was gone. Poor Toad shivered and tried to speak. But he only managed a groan.

"Toad!" barked Badger. "Enough of this nonsense! Explain yourself!"

"**Y**ou'd better calm down and start from the beginning," added Rat.

"You don't think Toad Hall's haunted, do you?" asked Toad afterwards. "Not that I'm, ahem, worried. But I thought you fellows might be."

"Indeed?" growled Badger, boldly leading the way into the library.

An uneasy Toad entered last.

"We'll soon get to the bottom of this," boomed Badger. "Aha!" He pointed to a ball rolling across the floor. Row upon row of books filled one entire wall. Below part of the bookshelf, a rug had been disturbed.

"H'm! There's more to this mystery than meets the eye," Badger frowned.

He began searching among shelves of dusty books that had not been moved in years. At last, Badger found a hidden lever. He gave it a firm tug. To the others' amazement, a secret door in the bookshelf swung open, stopping against the rug.

"I thought as much!" cried Badger.

Beyond the door, light filtered through a narrow window of frosted glass into a hidden, long-forgotten store-room. Inside, were two young, and far from ghostly, hedgehogs.

"Don't be cross, Mister Badger!" cried one, wearing a yellow cloak and hat. "My brother, Ben, and I were only playing."

"We've both been riding this rocking-horse," Ben added.

"I say!" cried Toad, eagerly springing onto the big, heavy, wooden horse and rocking wildly. Once again, its curved, rumbling runners shook the floor.

"There are other things here," said Ben, "like these few shiny buttons my sister, Daisy, found."

"They're old coins!" cried Rat.

"All this must be quite valuable," said Mole.

The hedgehogs took the others to a thick hedgerow, beyond Toad Hall.

"Our ball rolled in there and we found a tunnel," pointed Ben.

"It led to the hidden room through a trap-door," explained Daisy. "We shut the door behind us but it jammed."

"Then we discovered the bookshelf door," she continued. "We tried to slip out unseen that way. But we heard you all coming and hid again."

"I dropped our ball," added Tom.

"It was Daisy's cloak and hat I saw at the window," cried Toad. "They set me thinking!"

"You mean *shaking*!" teased Rat.

Soon the hedgehogs happily hurried off home with a large box of biscuits.

"They deserved a reward," smiled Toad. "I'll get them some new toys, too."

"We'll block up that tunnel first," frowned Badger. "We don't want any Wild Wooders sneaking into Toad Hall."

"Not a *ghost* of a chance!" chuckled Toad.

Special offer to our Wind In The Willows readers.

In every Wind In The Willows book produced by World International Ltd., you will find a special token. Collect six tokens and we will send you a super king size poster featuring all The Wind In The Willows characters.

<u>Return this page</u> together with your six tokens to:-

Marketing Dept, WITW, World International Ltd, Deanway Technology Centre, Wilmslow Road, Handforth, Cheshire, SK9 3FB

Your Name _____ Age _____

Address _____

_____

_____

_____ Postcode _____

Signature of Parent/Guardian _____

I enclose six tokens - please send me a Wind In The Willows poster.

We may occasionally wish to advise you of other Wind In The Willows gifts. If you would rather we didn't please tick this box. [ ]

Offer open to residents of UK, Channel Isles and Ireland only.

Collect six of these tokens
You will find one inside every
Wind in the Willows book which
has this special offer.

1
TOKEN

Titles in

The WIND in the WILLOWS COLLECTION

If you have any difficulty obtaining any of these books, please contact the
Marketing Department at:
World International Limited, Deanway Technology Centre,
Wilmslow Road, Handforth, Cheshire SK9 3FB
Telephone: 01625 650011